This 1989 edition published by Derrydale Books,
distributed by Crown Publishers, Inc.,
225 Park Avenue South
New York, N.Y. 10003

Directed by HELENA Productions Ltd.
Illustrated by Van Gool-Lefevre-Loiseaux

Produced by Twin Books
15 Sherwood Place
Greenwich, CT 06830

Printed and bound in Spain

ISBN 0-517-69319-4

hgfedcba

Printed in Spain by
Printer industria gráfica sa. Barcelona
D. L. B.: 26786-1989

Puss in Boots

DERRYDALE BOOKS
New York

Twin Books

Once upon a time in a village in a kingdom, there lived a miller and his three sons. Now, the miller's family always had enough to eat, but none to spare. One day, the old miller died, and he left his only possessions to his sons. To the oldest son he left his mill, to his middle son he left his donkey, and to his youngest son he left his cat. While the youngest son was fond of the cat, he felt that his father had not dealt fairly, for his brothers could earn a living with a mill and a donkey, but it seemed that little fortune could be made with a cat.

The youngest son was complaining to himself, when suddenly the cat spoke up. "Look here," it said quite plainly. "Get me a fine hat, cape and boots, and I'll see that your future will be bright."

So surprised was the young man to hear the cat speak that he obeyed at once. Taking his last coins, he went into the village and had the clothes especially made. The cat was as pleased as could be when he slipped on the boots, hat and cape. With a wave and a wink, he set off down the road, leaving his master to wonder if he'd been foolish to trust such an eccentric cat.

The cat, who soon came to be called Puss in Boots, wasted no time setting his plan into action. He stepped brightly along the road—stopping now and then only to adjust his hat, or wipe dust from his boots—until he came to a briar patch. There he lay down and pretended to be dead.

Curious at the sight of a cat so richly dressed, and wondering how he might have died there, a rabbit hopped out of the patch. No sooner had the rabbit sat down, when Puss in Boots jumped up and seized it by the ears.

Puss in Boots marched directly to the King's palace, where he boldly insisted on seeing the King at once.

Puss was escorted to the throne room, where he bowed deeply and presented the rabbit, saying, "Greetings, Your Majesty. My noble lord, the Marquis of Carabas, has sent me to deliver this gift to you personally." (The cat had just made up that name for the young man.)

"Please give your master my thanks," said the King graciously. As Puss was leaving, he heard the King asking the Princess if she was ready for their drive along the river.

Puss ran all the way back to his master, and instructed him to go at once to the river to bathe. When the young man questioned him, the cat said, "Trust me. Do as I say, and your future will be bright."

So he did as he was told, and was quite enjoying the water, when he saw the royal carriage approaching. Then he heard Puss shouting, "Help! The Marquis of Carabas is drowning! Help!"

When the King heard the familiar name, he ordered that the young man be rescued. "Sire," the cat whispered to the King, so as not to embarrass the Princess, "while my master was bathing, all his clothes were stolen." Puss had cleverly hidden his master's clothes, but the King couldn't know this, so he ordered a servant to fetch one of his finest suits. In no time at all the young man was dressed in a royal outfit that made him look so handsome that, with her father's permission, the Princess asked him to join them in the carriage.

Puss in Boots' job had only begun, however. The clever cat rushed down the road ahead of the carriage, until he came to a large field that the peasants were reaping. "Listen here!" he shouted. The peasants stopped to listen. "The royal carriage will be here shortly. When the King asks who owns these fields, you must tell him they are owned by the Marquis of Carabas, or you will be severely punished."

The peasants nodded agreement, afraid even to speak. "Now back to work with you!" ordered Puss.

Soon the royal party arrived, and the King ordered the carriage to stop. "Who owns these fields?" he called to the peasants.

Glancing nervously at the cat, the peasants replied, "The Marquis of Carabas owns all these fields, as far as you can see!"

"Ah!" said the King, leaning back in his seat. "And fine fields they are, young man."

The miller's son nodded and smiled, not knowing quite what to say. But the Princess took his silence for modesty, and was growing fonder of him by the minute.

24

The young man glanced out the window to see if Puss in Boots might give him some clue as to the nature of his plan, but the cat had already hurried away. Puss ran ahead of the carriage until he came to an enormous castle. The castle was owned by a dreaded ogre, who also owned all the fields along the road. The cat trotted across the drawbridge.

Upon his request, Puss in Boots was escorted to the ogre's chamber.

"Pardon me," said the cat, removing his hat with a flourish. "I had to make your acquaintance, having heard tell of your fame far and wide."

The ogre was flattered, but replied gruffly, "I've no time for vanities. What is it you want?"

"I have no doubt you are as fierce and brave as folks say," spoke Puss in Boots. "But I cannot believe the stories that you can transform yourself into anything you want."

"I shall prove I can do just that!" thundered the ogre. "And then you shall die as a reward for doubting one so great as I."

Before Puss in Boots could say another word, the ogre turned himself into a ferocious lion. The ogre's words dissolved into angry roars, and as he waved his huge paw in the air, the cat couldn't help noticing how large and sharp his claws were.

Puss was frightened nearly out of his boots, but quickly regained his composure. "If you please!" he shouted, to be heard above the roars. "That *is* as amazing a feat as I've ever seen. But I should think it quite impossible to change yourself into something as small as, say, a mouse." No sooner had he spoken the words, then the vain ogre turned himself into a tiny fieldmouse.

"Splendid!" cried Puss, clapping his paws together.

"And now I shall eat you!" cried the cat. As quick as a wink, Puss in Boots caught the mouse and ate him in one bite. Then he put on his hat, cleaned his whiskers, and made his way about the castle, sternly informing all the servants that they were soon to meet their new master.

Soon the royal carrige arrived, for the castle stood at the end of the road. Puss in Boots greeted the royal party at the gate. "Welcome to the castle of the Marquis of Carabas!" he exclaimed. "Perhaps you'd like some refreshment after your journey."

The King was delighted that his
new friend, whom his daughter
appeared to be very fond of, lived
in such a splendid castle.

"My house is your house," said
the young man with a humble bow.

The group went into the Great Hall, where a cold banquet had been quickly prepared by order of the cat. The King proposed that the Marquis marry his daughter, and when the happy couple agreed, they lifted their glasses in a merry toast.

A lavish wedding was planned for the Marquis and the Princess, who were so obviously in love. No one in the kingdom could doubt that it was a joyous event, for on the day of the wedding, all the bells in the land rang out the good tidings. Lords and peasants alike were invited to the wedding, in which Puss in Boots played a part by proudly holding the Princess' train.

No one was more surprised at the wedding than the groom's brothers, to whom the new Prince promised land and wealth. When the brothers asked how he had come to his fortune, he winked and replied, "I'll explain later."

As for Puss in Boots, after three days of wedding festivities, he thought he should be very happy to spend the rest of his days chasing mice and pretending that he was just an ordinary cat.